Little Bear and Emily

THE NEW NEIGHBOUR

A story of friendship ...

Text by Florence Ducatteau
Illustrated by Chantal Peten

PLURUS

Oliver, the little bear, lives in the middle of the countryside, far away from everyone else.

He’s quite happy living on his own with just his thoughts and toys for company. He enjoys fishing and playing with his raft. He doesn’t need anybody else.

Then, one day, Oliver receives a letter on the doormat. It is from a girl who has just moved in to a cottage nearby. She tells him her name is Emily.

Emily asks if she could come over to play. Oliver really is not very happy. ‘I’m very happy with the way things are, and, anyway, I don’t like girls !’ he says to himself, grumpily. So he doesn’t write back.

The next day, when Oliver gets up in the morning, he spots another pink envelope sitting on the doormat. It is another letter from Emily.

‘Oh bother!’ he says to himself. ‘She obviously likes very girly things like pink writing paper and hearts. Yuk!’

'If she thinks I am going to answer her letter she is very much mistaken,' he says to himself as he sits in his boat. Then it starts to rain. 'Oh, bother,' he says to himself.

Oliver is very unsettled by Emily's letters and starts to think about them far too much. 'Why does she keep writing to me?' he asks himself. 'And on top of that it is still raining.'

Oliver finds it difficult to forget all the letters he has received. He now has a neighbour. What should he do? He goes out fishing at his favourite spot.

‘Good morning,’ says a voice and there is Emily, also holding a fishing rod.

Oliver is not very happy. This is his spot for fishing. ‘Go away,’ he mutters angrily, ‘this is where I fish!’
‘Look out,’ says Emily,’our lines are tangled.’

‘You look out,’ shouts Oliver. ‘You don’t even know how to fish properly. Find your own spot.’

‘Of course I know how to fish,’ says Emily. ‘You’re the one who doesn’t know how….’
Oops they both fall in.

Emily starts to laugh and she laughs so loud and for so long that eventually even grumpy old Oliver cannot help himself and he starts laughing too. She points at him and laughs.
'We are both soaking wet !'

They both climb out and put their soaking clothes out in the sun to dry.
'That sun is really warm,' says Emily and Oliver agrees.
'Would you like to play a game?' asks Emily.
'Yes, I think I would,' says Oliver.

‘Let’s see who can skim the water with a pebble the best,’ says Oliver.

‘OK,’ says Emily and she seems to be quite good at it. That surprises Oliver.

‘Do you like watching dragon flies?’ asks Oliver.
‘I don’t know,’ says Emily. ‘What are dragon flies?’
‘Look, they are just above are heads. Aren’t they wonderful?’
‘Yes,’ says Emily, ’they are.’
‘Will you come back tomorrow?’
asks Oliver, shyly.
Emily smiles, ‘Yes, I will.’